MY TEACHER for PRESIDENT

by Kay Winters   illustrated by Denise Brunkus

PUFFIN BOOKS

To Dr. Richard Creasey, a superintendent who encouraged and valued
the work of the teachers in the Palisades School District
K.W.

. . . and Linda Pratt for vice president!
D.B.

PUFFIN BOOKS
Published by the Penguin Group
Penguin Young Readers Group, 345 Hudson Street, New York, New York 10014, U.S.A.
Penguin Group (Canada), 90 Eglinton Avenue East, Suite 700, Toronto, Ontario, Canada M4P 2Y3 (a division of Pearson Penguin Canada Inc.)
Penguin Books Ltd, 80 Strand, London WC2R 0RL, England
Penguin Ireland, 25 St Stephen's Green, Dublin 2, Ireland (a division of Penguin Books Ltd)
Penguin Group (Australia), 250 Camberwell Road, Camberwell, Victoria 3124, Australia (a division of Pearson Australia Group Pty Ltd)
Penguin Books India Pvt Ltd, 11 Community Centre, Panchsheel Park, New Delhi - 110 017, India
Penguin Group (NZ), 67 Apollo Drive, Rosedale, North Shore 0632, New Zealand (a division of Pearson New Zealand Ltd)
Penguin Books (South Africa) (Pty) Ltd, 24 Sturdee Avenue, Rosebank, Johannesburg 2196, South Africa

Registered Offices: Penguin Books Ltd, 80 Strand, London WC2R 0RL, England

First published in the United States of America by Dutton Children's Books, a division of Penguin Young Readers Group, 2004
Published by Puffin Books, a division of Penguin Young Readers Group, 2008

1 3 5 7 9 10 8 6 4 2

Text copyright © Kay Winters, 2004
Illustrations copyright © Denise Brunkus, 2004
All rights reserved

THE LIBRARY OF CONGRESS HAS CATALOGED THE DUTTON CHILDREN'S BOOKS EDITION AS FOLLOWS:
Winters, Kay.
My teacher for President / by Kay Winters; [illustrations by Denise Brunkus].—1st ed.   p.   cm.
Summary: A second-grader writes a television station with reasons why his teacher would make a good president, but only if she can continue teaching till the end of the year.
ISBN: 0-525-47186-3 (hc)
[1. Teachers—Fiction. 2. Schools—Fiction.] I. Brunkus, Denise, ill. II. Title.
PZ7.W7675My 2004 [E] 2 22 2003019222

Puffin Books ISBN 978-0-14-241170-4

Designed by Gloria Cheng
Manufactured in China

Dear Channel 39,

I saw on TV that elections are coming.

At school we have been learning about the president's job.

My teacher would be just right!

Let me know what you think.

My teacher loves white houses.

She's used to being followed everywhere.

When my teacher walks into a room,
people pay attention.

My teacher goes to lots of meetings.

And she's always signing important papers.

My teacher acts quickly when there's an emergency.

And she says health care is important.

My teacher likes to go on trips.

President Robbins travels through Egypt.

President Robbins enjoys Paris.

President Robbins walks the Great Wall of China.

She deals with the media every day.

My teacher would be good for the country.

She wants to clean up the Earth.

She finds jobs for people.

She is a good listener.

She believes in peace.

Love, Oliver

P.S. Just make sure she doesn't leave before the end of the year.